Flying Lesson

Selected Poems

PAULETTE JILES

Toronto
Oxford University Press
1995

Oxford University Press
70 Wynford Drive, Don Mills, Ontario M3C 1J9

Oxford New York
Athens Auckland Bangkok Bombay
Calcutta Cape Town Dar es Salaam Delhi
Florence Hong Kong Istanbul Karachi
Kuala Lumpur Madras Madrid Melbourne
Mexico City Nairobi Paris Singapore
Taipei Tokyo Toronto

and associated companies in
Berlin Ibadan

Oxford is a trademark of Oxford University Press

to my aunts
Max Racy Wayant
Mayme Racy Townsend
and
Marcia Jiles Lieurance

Canadian Cataloguing in Publication Data
Jiles, Paulette, 1943-
    Flying lesson: selected poems

ISBN 0-19-541097-1

I. Title.

PS8569.I5F58 1995   C811'.54   C95-931935-2
PR9199.3.J55F58 1995

Copyright © Paulette Jiles 1995
1 2 3 4 - 98 97 96 95
Cover design: Heather Delfino
This book is printed on permanent (acid-free) paper ∞ .
Printed in Canada

POETRY REVIEW

There are so many new poets we have to
watch in the near future;

afterwards their silences go off like guns.
We want to hear more from these people and
their deceptive, inexpensive art

we hope they stay out of jail,
that they might tell us of the odd corners
of this country (for which we have few

references) as well as the hotels of Spain
(which are familiar, at least in print)
and their one big thought which may

occur in the mulligan of dreams,
if only they can remember, if only
among the things they write

under *To Do Today* poetry will be
listed; remember the semi-divine
beings with feathers and robes who

leap out of hedges
bearing exultant flashlights
on their way to an earthquake;

wrestle with them, break
their thighs, do not let them go until you have
their addresses, we want

to hear more from these beings.

FLYING LESSON

These are the wings of the airplane.
They have leading edges and cut the air
like a pie-knife through a fine meringue.

These are the struts. They hold the wings to the fuselage;
they correspond to the arms of angels
that you see in ancient paintings,
held out in surprise or warning
against wings with feathers
and no leading edges.

These are the cowlings that cover the engines
and then the propellers,
sun-dogs, solar discs, which will drag behind them
the boxy fuselage
full of passengers, babies, canned vegetables
the nurse says we must eat,
sheets of plexiglass, sleeping bags,
a roll of plastic pipe and the rest of us.

These are the skis on which we take off,
smashing across the raftered ice,
their shock absorbers fed up with all this,
both propellers tuned coarse and driving
at the clear air like diamond drills
reaching for altitude, for distance
and a tailwind out of the north.

Kiss off, kiss off, O earth,
O village of earth-folk down below
waving your puffy-mitt goodbyes,
we are the people of the air.
Here the milk of winter clouds
is churned into our special butter.

Some day when the roads come in
and cars like armadillos
lurch up their frozen byways,
remember we once flew like legends in these frail kites.
Remember us, a boreal airborne royalty.
Remember some of us died.

And these are the dials of the flight deck.
This is the vertical speed indicator,
this is the radar, hissing in green sweeps,
the oil pressure and the bank-and-turn.
This is the altimeter which tells us of the earth,
now drawing up in a snowy flow,

where we owe a life, despite the aviation of souls.
We return in our damp fur and parkas
toward an artificial horizon,

to everything that is unjust, unpaid-for and unwarranted,
claimed by our bodies like baggage;
we, the earth-people,
descend again.

WINDIGO

No one understands the Windigo. His voice
is like the white light of hydrogen, only long.
Some say he carries his head under his arm, for
others it's the race down to the rapids
where the canoes must draw close to the shore
and he jumps in. You have time for a few last words.

Under the moon he turns pearl grey, the
head chatters amiably about meals. He is the
Hungry Man, the one who reached this wasteland
of the soul and did not emerge. Not whole. Not as you
would recognize wholeness.

Sometimes he wants to be killed, putting his
heart or what there is of it in the way of arrows,
bullets, he wants his soul or what there is of it
to spring heavenward to the village where people
begin again, he too
wants to cross the bridge.
His story is one who reached starvation
and death and did not make it through, not
as you would recognize making it.
People shoot the Windigo, they
do not pray for him, or it.

NORTHERN REPORTER

Nothing can jar me from this attentive position
this pen hesitating over the paper
is a cardiogram needle
the page will be full of spikes
and indications.

   You have been held hostage, have you?
Men with knives
this came after the bullet
through the window and everyone
tried to get in the bathtub.
   Don't worry, my dear, it is their hormones,
they will be taken to jail
and in there
they will have to hold other men hostage
instead of nurses
and the consequences will be worse.
You say you are leaving this goddamned north,
this Frontier City?
Good, I will write that down.
I have no arguments,
only quotes.

Elder Wapiquae will tell me about stars,
this is for the young people
who are forgetting the traditions of their ancestors,
she says they run around and drink
and throw knives at each other.

'Write down what I say. There are three stars together at breakup
time in the spring, they are the man who holds the stern paddle
of the universe. Sometimes he is there and then he disappears. He
is erratic. The Bow Paddler is the north star, he stays steady.
In between them in the cosmic vessel are all the stories of the world.'

   I will make sure you appear just as you are
in our pages, no distortion, the hostages, the elder,
those at the wild rice camps and loons and stars.
And all this time (I am sitting here)
my heart is talking to itself,
all its valves and dull arterial thuds,
it is a high-ranking defector,
   under all this nodding and quotes it says,
Listen to me. Only to me. Listen.

LIVING ALONE

The earth folds up her grasses.
Starshine strikes like the appearance of aliens.
The aurora is a piano, playing blues
in green neon. The junked taxi sinks
into the asters.

In the centre of all this noisy brilliance
is a cabin; silence and absence.

Sometimes you spoon-feed the soul,
silence in small sips,
a sort of dole, you
put it on relief.

Foxtail grass turns gravely on its spears.
Shut up, wait for the angel or the airplane
disguised as an angel to descend
with silent twin propellers out of the
madonna-blue evening, wait for
your cue, your
moment to appear in the
zodiacal footlights of
this special and dreadful
one-man show.

THROUGH THE BURN

A door opened to another world
and a blue heron flew out.

A canoe sailed into the epicentre
and turned to glass.

The film that runs always in the brain stalls and burns
its image. Trees fell into ovens, a design in black

was fired onto the face of the earth, and over this water,
this solution of ash and acid, we travel between

the pages of a new world, filling in blanks, voices (where
there were none) noises (where the wind pulls a long note

of silence through black flutes.)

AIR ACCIDENT REPORT

From these deaths of fog and machinery
   we hope to excuse ourselves.
Your news arrives on the wings of voices.
   We are awakened from our daily bath.

In the metal confetti
which was the airplane,
   the village people walk around confused,
their lives in their hands.
   Pieces of instruments lay hopeless in the snow.
In this there is neither
   philosophy nor solutions,
only loss; four children, two adults.
Something arrived in the air

like a revelation,
and then disintegrated.
It happened too fast to understand what was said
or meant
and it was not in our language.

It is not in any language.
For years they will piece together small events,
looking for clues,
the conclusions will be bound and distributed,
they think they know already. So do we,

but no one will second-guess
what might be found
in these hard-bound volumes of snow and gasoline
and fire.
O pilot error, the last judgement.

NIGHT FLIGHT TO ATTIWAPISKAT

We are flying directly into darkness, the
dim polestar rides on the starboard wing,
Orion and his blue gems freeze in the southwest.

Our rare and singular lives are in the hands of the pilot:
after him, the radar and one engine.
There were two engines when we started out
but the other one died.

We watch the starboard propeller feather
in slow, coarse revolutions.
The pilot says we will make Attiwapiskat or some place.
    Icarus, our pilot and our downfall.

We would become angels and not pay the price.
Two thousand feet below, dim lakes pour past
in white sheets as if on their way to a Laundromat.
How could we have sunk so low?
At times like this I consider life after death
as if it were a binary system;
there are no half-lives.
We track cautiously down the Milky Way,
the home of nebulae and Cygnus.

We are footloose in the corridors of the aurora.

The long stream of my life is flying out
behind this airplane like skywriting
on the subarctic night, fluttering,
whipped with urgency.
Each episode was always cut off from the last,
I used to find myself a series of hostile strangers,
startled in doorways.

Now they gather themselves up,
the person who was a wife, a daughter, a friend, a victim,

a perpetrator, a person with a pen and another carrying
a blank mask, the last one at present
at the cleaners.

They catch up and slam together like
a deck of cards, packed into the present
moment.
I draw one out; it's the ace of airplanes.

The radar repeats a fixed,
green idea. The pilot feels for the radio touch
of Thunder Bay.

At a thousand feet lower we make quick decisions
about our loyalties, the other engine might fail,
the suitcases of our hearts might be opened,
with all that contraband,
the jewels and screams;
we might have things to declare.
The universe is my native country
poetry is my mother tongue
the ideas I have purchased on this side
of the border don't amount to more than
a hundred dollars.

What comes after this?
What do you mean, what comes after this?
This is it.
Attiwapiskat approaches, a Cree village
on a cold salt coast, flying patchwork quilts
in several more colours than are found in nature,
shining with blue-white runway lights.

We will sleep in the guesthouse tonight,
that refuge of displaced persons.
The pilot will go down and replace the valve
and say nothing happened.

(But we flew into darkness at the rim of the world
where distant lights broke through
and something failed us.
Then at the edge when we were stamped
and ready to go through, we were turned back)

We can unload and forget it.
But I will remember
and then go back and forget again.
This is Attiwapiskat, everything is as it should be.
We slide down to the airstrip through salt fogs
from Hudson Bay that slip through the night
like airborne bedsheets.
We get off, still life with sleeping bags.
Approaching us is an earthman,
speaking Cree.

CHRONOLOGY BEGINS

Chronology begins with the stars.
It is fall, the Seven Sisters rise above
the evening and the geese have already
gone to Mexico in shattered lines.

No I am not coming back, not
even in the spring. Let's not
call each other.
Who has time for these things?
Arguments and debts?
We might go out and die
among the asters. Already
there have been two car wrecks,
   one near Dinorwic and the other
turned over and over into
the Sturgeon River. The Seven Sisters

are an old, bright fatality, which has
reached the world of anti-matter,
   net-floats in space
   The Bear's Head, *Makwa-estguan.*

   The time we have now is winter time,
the sun is a rare occurrence, we are
wasting minutes in these
arguments over the phone,
with a three-second delay,
echoing.

NORTHERN RADIO

The mind recuperates from the day slowly,
from sleep, it takes a while.
Slowly turning in its nest at night it wonders,
yes, it wonders, it has its
doubts.

The brain is something else. In the
morning it turns on like a lightbulb
the tongue like a pull-chain unleashing it
prepared for the radio-shack and the powder snow.
Turn on the transmitter, broadcast brain-music.

The mind is more admirable and more bruised.
Sometimes it will not appear at all,
sluggish and offended. There is nothing you can
offer it but the situation.
The brain is happy with anything.

SHE WRITES IN SPANISH TO SOMEONE SHE KNEW

She writes in Spanish to someone she knew, but she never knew him very well at all. At her side are a list of words that are supposed to mean what she wants to say, along with a picture of the last time she saw him and a Coleman lamp. *I am far away*, she writes, importantly. All over the village lamps are coming on, people turn up their evening mentality and light themselves, they shine around card games and food.

Actually, I am not so far away, she writes. *I am extremely close.*

MY SLEEPING BAG

My sleeping bag used to belong to a pilot
who crashed near here,
and was buried in the south.
He was young, they say.
He was flying in on Christmas Eve.
I didn't know this when I bought it.
It seems to still want to fly away
into dreams and remote, starry holidays
it is still stained with gas and oil which
airplane wrecks splash out for hundreds
of yards around.
It came to me half-price,
looking for a new owner, the hieroglyphs of disaster
written on its zipper bag in
engine oil.
Come here and I'll hold you, I said:
we lay wrapped on the cabin floor
all night at bush camp.

The northern lights flared, they made
searchlights looking throughout Lyra in Scorpio
for the plane.
I coughed badly in the early morning
like a faulty engine.
People emerged from my dreaming speaking
perfect Cree
the voices of the living woke me and we landed safely
alive again.

NIGHT FEARS

1.) There is something in the dishwater
and it is stirring and moving, a grey
     microthing becoming macro

2.) The woodstove fire is eating through some secret place
and will burn bigger after I fall asleep

3.) Voices are coming from under the lake outside
they are discussing entries into the cabin

4.) bears   bears   bears

a friend says, how could you live there
all by yourself
     I could never do it
well I'm not interested if you could never do it
I hate this hand-to-breast wide-eyed
I'm-more-feminine-and-weak-than-you-are stuff
of course you could never do it
neither could I but
     here I am
making poems out of
night fears.

IN THE LEGENDS

In the legends, it's always like this;
still water, one person alone on a beach,
　oppositions silently sliding
on each other like the two arguments
of an earthquake,
its inevitable faults.
The mountains move in and out of clouds
like secret doctrines.
Red willows line up on the sand,
not speaking to one another,
and like this they have spent the night,
and the morning,
and their entire lives.

After long silence, speech appears
like a voice from a red willow bush, burning.
I love you, or
the bread pans are on that shelf, or
I am afraid of dying.

At one in the morning,
poetry fastens with clean, urgent hands
on my nightgown, saying
Say this, say this, this is
the perfect thing to say.
And then whole lines arrive,
whispering modestly,
Say me.

WINTER NIGHT ON THE RIVER

Dreams with long horns and handsfull of messages
sparkling like frost wait until nightfall.

Our skulls are woodstoves and around this heat
vast, transparent people gather, vital and strange.

The cabin is dipped in darkness, tie-dyed.
Only the red from the woodstove grate and reflections

from tin plates escape. Sirius picks at the window.
Diapers wave at half-mast, desperately clean.

The children watch the insides of their eyes.
Things will be revealed in dreams to them,

economy-sized revelations, tiny ideas.

The body shuts down. Hot pine ticks in the stove.
We sleep because we have to dream, as when

we are awake we must speak. Speech and dreams;
behind the banner of these old imperatives we

have marched for two million years, to what
(unspeakable) end? On the banks of the Pipestone

River and the subarctic night; and now one of the
children calls out sharply, ambushed by dreams.

ONCE AT NIGHT I WAS STOPPED BY A COMET

   This is the country of the sky, dilating
stars pull brilliance from outer space,
   green curtains slide across
a mysterious scene; the borealis and its
moonshow.

   Once at night I was stopped by a comet
I saw it blow up in green splinters.
It was north of 54°.
'This is life in the remote interior' I said
to myself, and the shards extinguished separately
as they fell.

   We grow accustomed to pure hallucination.
The mind is an eye, it knows something
   it tells only in dreams
   (an arctic ocean breaking over frozen
bicycles, fireflies flash in the winter night, a
blacktail deer stands in the white drifts saying
   this is your mind).

FORTY BELOW

   The birch has red cores that spring free
like cinnamon sticks; out of the white
   frozen interior
   my axe strikes flakes of blue fire.

You can't hesitate on nights like this
   the dogs shift and beg at the door
like the part of myself that would hesitate
be fragile and at rest
   (you can't leave us out here like this)

moisture gels in the air and drifts down
like star-chips hammered from Orion.

The fuel is consumed and the blows
of the frosted axe throw white shards
like snowbirds, flying and flying.

The slow, clear cold of the subarctic
mails white letters beneath the unlocked door.

SEARCH AND RESCUE
For Staff Sergeant Ab Boley

I
This is a cedar swamp. He is in here somewhere
on aluminum snowshoes, a fresh trail and clouds
of nicotine streaming behind like smoke flares.

Searching for lost children (some ran away), drunks falling
into ravines, midnight farmers out loose in the sleet-
slick fields in search of suicide, a man with a shotgun
and eyes full of firepower. There are
his clues.

He moves on the edges like a roll of dimes or
something hungry. There are false starts,
midnight alarms. He lives

for the moment he talks the gun away from the
suicide man, a flash of chequered shirt at the
bottom of a ravine, the second when the child
in the clearing turns and cries out,
still alive.

The drunk and the suicide and the Roadhouse
Mystery Killer are erratic and snakey, they are
the gothics, the hates and divorces, moon revenges.
They are petrified of the dog. These people could be
anywhere, but he always
finds the child exactly in the centre of the world.

II
What if you were lost in this cedar swamp,
you would shout and then scream, after a while
you would become childlike, you would forget
all the numbers

that have been assigned to you, your
telephone number, social insurance, driver's
licence, the arguments with your loved one
would evaporate, you would forget your first
name and then your last name,

and every direction would be the wrong one and so
directions would cease. You would be at the hub
of the universe, and around you, in every direction,
the world. As you finally give up hope, you
become the eye
of creation.

Then he would arrive, crashing through the
rigid, thorned sticks, bringing with him
all the numbers, the arguments, the first
and last names, your identity whether you
want it or not.

Maybe you don't want it anymore. He knows
this. He has found lots of children. When
the sergeant goes home at dawn he looks like
he has just come back from the centre of the earth,

the hard way,
by way of a town called Argus, in Egremont
Township, where all the murderers live.

RAGTIME
a Series Of Poems
Concerning
Mr Scott Joplin,
'King Of The Ragtime Composers'
Of
Sedalia, Missouri
and
Tom Turpin's Rosebud Cafe
St Louis, Missouri

I THE SPORTING LIFE

He gets up at dawn and moves
quietly around the room to the first
bars of the music, unrested and troubled.
Weeping Willow, Sugar-Cane Rag
the sound of people being entertained at their leisure
and the sound of the entertainers,
the women with confused dreams, elite
syncopations,
the dense metal arguments of cattle cars
in the background draining the air of sense.
He offers everything he has with just this
desire or private longing held in reserve:
   (and the whole day, twenty miles away,
   the River will slide southwards
   through cottonwood and revetment dikes
   the water like alloys hammered and tin,
   its thin surface moving around
   Slaughterhouse Bend)
that one would wake up tomorrow
morning in a familiar place
rested and untroubled.

In the section of the city where there are warehouses
in the part of town where you can find chophouses,
neon, steam, ducks and squid hung up by their voices,

languages and porcelain packed in straw
he moves restlessly,
   drapes thrown shut against the noise
of the invented world
   a woman half-sleeping.
The mind and its complaints sometimes
   cannot be silenced.
His long, precise hands move objects here
and there;
   her earrings, a series of maps,
   the imagined music:
   Solace, A Mexican
   Serenade.

II THE BIOGRAPH RECORDING BLP 1006Q

Here is the *Maple Leaf* with its odd hesitations,
and maybe only *Weeping Willow* is Joplin's playing
with the walking bass scored light as streaks
of rain on window glass
the light of dawn like metal
and, outside, the noise of the city even at
this hour noisy as barrelhouse, with
shouting down alleyways.
He leaves her earrings on the map so she
will not forget either the maps or the earrings
or the fragile skill of listening
to the speech that lies hidden in
the strange cartography of thought;
he gets up out of the tangled sheets and moves
quietly through the overture of sunrise
drawing the curtains so
the light will not wake her but
she is already awake, laid up
in the drifts of pillows, shoaled,
half-dreams like the serious and attentive
entertainment of ragtime,
this ragged time.

Joplin playing until dawn in Sedalia,
the sound of cattle cars crashing in from Texas,
the tenderloin with its ornate, tragic night life,
his nails pale as champagne, playing
Something Doing and *Grace and Beauty.*

We need somebody to look out for us,
to leave our earrings where they can be found,
to draw the curtain against the rainy
acid light;
and at the moment of waking we repair ourselves,
our lives like piano rolls, cranky and shot with pauses,
punched full of minute holes so that
we may carry with us this inaudible music,
gracenotes, the springing joy of a walking bass.

Even when we wake up and are afraid to wake up
when we can't sleep and are afraid still
of the larger world that lies in sleep
and the music of bars comes smoking up
out of the long chutes of downtown streets
with dirty weather at dawn and bright
streaks coursing down the glass
and something troubling the very air of the planet
there is the formal, steadfast grace
of *Weeping Willow,*
and Joplin's hand set to it,
clean as rain.

III LILY QUEEN; THE GIFT

Somebody has been good to you.
Somebody has given you a stone and a feather
and taught you a certain melody.
Somebody promised you California and you got it.
You won at three-card monte.

You inherited a large parcel of bottomland
along a major river.
At times everything implodes and disintegrates,
carrying all the structures downwards but then
you remember you own California.
Somebody laid beside your head, when
you were sleeping, a wonderful device
and every night of your life it is wound up again
and it ticks with precise jewels,
a thing of wonder.

With clean, deft precision Joplin sets out *Pineapple Rag*
because he doesn't know what else to call it.
Sometimes we are in love with an unnamed force
and we don't know what to call it,
and people say, *What is this bright thing*
that shines in you hand?
What is this concise, formal music
that came out of bordellos?

And when Joplin was bruised and foundered
by the heavy life that moved down on him
like a sorghum press,
extinguishing, relentless,
how could he respond but with these
luminous landslides of notes,
with *Elite Syncopations, Heliotrope Bouquet*?
Somebody had been good to him
a woman from Texarkana
leaving him with a very subtle, very fatal gift.
He shuts out the uncoloured world, the alleyways
down which the cluttered shouting of men
moving boxes of lettuce and soft drinks
litters the silence,
and the city disappears
and with it all the speech of strangers.

IV THE ENTERTAINERS

I am not sure we do not apprentice to the devil
for the voices we desire.
The audiences are suspicious and weighty,
and people who move from city to city
are often in trouble with themselves,
petulant, furious, nobody can find the ice,
we hear ourselves telling the same story once more,
we become our own impatient audience
suspicious and weighty
wondering what we have paid to hear
this yet again,
and then at dawn everything is perfectly clear,
light as tissue.
Within moments you will walk out of the room
or say something in another language
of which I only know a few phrases.
There is all around the barrel light lancing
through the curtains, your
love of distant rivers, the speech of strangers.
Somebody has been good to you,
promising as California.

Look like you always look, act normal,
never let them see you are afraid
of either the future or the past.
When you wake up and are reluctant to wake up,
when you can't sleep and are afraid still
of the larger world that plots itself in sleep
with its giant people, flat as major arcana
—The Lovers, The Prophetess—
splashing up out of the mica-white river
at Slaughterhouse Bend, electric with
lunatic, thrilling news, saying to you
    What is it?

Somebody gets up and throws the curtains
in a gesture both secret and efficient,
rain melts the city into a running series
of neon streams
thin as an early conversation,
and sits carefully on the bed and asks,
   What is it?

V SEDALIA

Training himself not to think
   because there is nothing to think
   in words
not in all this noise, the dense, smoky rooms,
or when it is silent or nearly so at 5 a.m.
and the engines of the Katy pitch down the track
wooing the Storyville of Sedalia with disjoined notes
—its endearing, feckless charge and pause and
impatient halt at the thick, bricky station,
the people getting on,
buttered by coal-oil lamplights.

And because there is nothing to think in words
he plays the music that will attract and betray
him to strangers
   (*I didn't know a coloured man could compose like that*)
the bright expenditure of hands upon the keys
describing our hot, smoky interiors,
or the rooms of deep cool that lie in our hearts
the shining, punctual brasses of laughter,
the return of the major theme, busted souls,
hearts worn down like upholstery and springs,
the deliberate, restrained, precise notations
of the score.

He would have stood for hours at a rainy window
busy with the rich accumulation of thought
the increase and assemblage

of these structures
   (the rain, the earrings, the maps,
   the grace, the beauty, the solace)

   Rain drifts over the town
   like a long salting
   the questions and more questions
   unanswered and adrift;

Where have we come from
   (*besides Texarkana*)
and was it for this we were born?
   (*Yes; for this*)

Even at the last when his hands shook
and could not be laid to the keys,
when his eyes became the confined, pure blank
of coins spent on damp counters
in a remote city
and a pigeon drifted down
through his ruining memory
like a mottled, triangular rag
he recalls that this love, and this music was
born in a cathouse in Sedalia.

And because he could not be thought to think
or compose operas
his big, vital love pours out in ragtime
a sort of spiritual vaudeville
luminous with pranks and gracenotes
eccentric triplets
startling ride-outs,
his heroine this woman
of mysterious parentage;
Lily Queen
Eugenia
Leola, and *Solace*
A Mexican
Serenade.

VI STOPTIME RAG

Didn't your Sunday shoes ever dance
of their own accord?
Haven't any herons moved heartlessly past
your rivers and shores?
Do you not possess either river or shores,
has your watch not told you
Now is the time
ticking with precise jewels,
haven't you ever entered a strange city
with the intention of buying squid and ducks
and brandy,
learned a few words of Chinese,
    laid hands on a musical instrument,
drawn startling promises and prophesies
    out of an ocarina
with your very breathing,
    melted with surrendering joy before
some object he has left behind,
    become unhinged, possessed
with the startling possibility that this structured
    brain would reach *Stoptime* and
in the pauses the piano would continue playing
like ornate piercing
springing liberal and uncounted notes,
your Sunday shoes dancing by themselves
    right out of the closet?

VII CARRIE GOES TO KANSAS CITY
(A Rag By Tom Turpin)

He is light as water
    fluctuating as a candle-flame in the wind
of a passing skirt,
    he plays around with old scores
something told him to arrive here
    alive and whole
the city fractures into daytime

    human agency impels
the silence out of alleyways
    strange lists are made up in kitchens
of whatever gets them
    through the day
they have conspired in public places
    pretended to act normal
got away with it
    indulged in espionage
met once in a monastery
    laundered money
got away with it
    she wears fake pearl earrings
she tells people they are inherited
    that somebody has been good to her
that she owns California

    she gets away with it

VIII   THE ASTROLOGER AT THE STATE FAIR IN SEDALIA

Do not hold the cards too tightly,
they warm themselves at living hands, they want flesh.
They became, at one time in the distant past,
too perfectly drawn and abstract; The Prophetess,
The Lovers. They began to brace up an imagined
world with such strict disapprovals, such
precise conduct that their world turned entirely
to paper; and now they want emotions, ragtime,
your joyfulness. They are the enemies you have imagined.
Do not give any money to the man who panhandles
at the entrance to the fairgrounds, he is not
who he appears to be, pass on by.
Avoid any invitation that comes on a printed card.
Give generously, but not to the wrong person.
What person?
How can you know what person?
There is no method of knowing.
It is a good thing you have come to me.

I am a gateway.
The Other World can only be turned into experience
by money. The right kind of money.
Not just any money.

I am a gateway.
Within this card lies an overmastering love or desire
—I can't tell which, neither can you—
but neither love nor desire will ever come
(dancing like Sunday shoes
   logical as ragtime)
if you continue to fear and enjoy it.
Spend it all.
You will meet a long journey, you will take
a pale man—of what height I can't tell—
but do not go into any establishment on
the riverfront, stay where you are, you may
become a representative species. Avoid
abstraction. Rotate your tires. The cards tell
what crosses you; it is both
l'envie and *la tendresse* and also *peur*.
I have been asked to give you
an enigmatic message; go soon to
Slaughterhouse Bend at Mile 213 on the Missouri,
above the mouth of the Lamine; your cousin
from Sedalia has asked to meet you there
at the cave you both know. These are family
matters. Always keep your pearl earrings close
to hand even though they are both fake.
When caught, lie or confess, whichever
is most convenient.
You will find the real earrings placed
on a series of maps.
Decipher the maps, it
is most important, it is
urgent, vital, your
life depends on it.
Spend it all.

THE GRIFFON POEMS

In 1679, the explorer La Salle, attempting to find a route to Indian or Cathay, built on Lake St Clair a small ship which he named The Griffon.

He and his captain and crew sailed into Lake Huron and through the straits of Mackinak. They continued on to the southern shores of Lake Michigan. There La Salle, Father Louis Hennepin, and others, left the ship and continued down the Illinois River to the Mississippi. La Salle left the ship with orders that they were to return to Lake St Clair.

The last sighting of the ship was reported by Father Hennepin.

They set sail on the 18th of September 1679 from (the mouth of the Illinois) with a very favourable light west wind, making their adieu by firing a single cannon. And we were never able afterwards to learn what course they had taken, and though there is no doubt but what she perished, we were never able to learn any other circumstances of their shipwreck.

There is some evidence that a ship of The Griffon's age was wrecked on Russel Island, near Tobermory, off the Bruce Peninsula, in Georgian Bay.

I LIFE IN THE WILDERNESS

There is no time to kill and so we don't talk much.
The lakes here have their own systems and currents run

on time, you have to catch them. Like blue pipelines
under water they have someplace to go, carrying supplies.

The Griffon with a fat spritsail bends toward the surface
as if to scoop up water, prevailing westerlies winding

through the clear air, which we package with these sails
and draw. Everything here is whole, unlike home where we were

handed our life piecemeal; everything was piecemeal; here, this
country is open to anybody, these great virgin

everythings, and the angel with the sword far away and not
a baron in sight. Let's pretend we are inhuman, nobody

will know, among these shores like palaces, the cliffs and
towers, on this clean water we walk with our great sails.

We could pretend to be gods if we knew how a god acted,
if we could divine how a god speaks, if we understood

the motivations of gods. At this place the earth's stone
heart shows, like painted Jesus and his picturesque

interior. The red blood of granite islands, torn pines.
Let's keep sailing, somebody will figure it out. A god

has only one personality, they say, and that is force.
One-dimensional, flat, he is a force on the water.

Geese fly through the sparkling rain.

This is life in the wilderness; hungry.
This is life as a force; uncomplicated.

II THE BOSUN, NIGHT WATCH

Long ago (the bosun tells himself a story) an
exploding star became a lighthouse, somewhere
to the left of the equator.

Solar winds blew its hair around.
After such a birth,
what kind of life awaits it?

My mast draws circles around
the lighthouse-star
waves comb themselves out, we are

running northwestwards down
an unknown coast. O nocturnal
ballads, ship of the auroral ocean,

we are marked with moon spots. I feel
the rush of water lay
on the rudder like a deep snake, the
tiller shakes.

Left and right
the red and green running lights

shine through glass walls of fresh water.
Sailing is one of the
varieties of love, it is one of the

varieties of solitude, it is prayer-dancing
with the new world.
Language has flown away from me in one of

the varieties of devotion to water. To
devotion, to
lighthouses.

III THE WOMAN ON THE BOWSPRIT

I live on the prow of The Griffon
dressed in copper bands, a
woman of salt and cedar.

I am pure decoration, like a hood
ornament.

Life here on The Griffon's nose
is variable. I was carved
by a master carver in Montreal,
a sort of chiselling obstetrician.
He gave me form, it was his
thick hands I sprang from, shedding
chips and shavings. Men instinctively
like me, and no wonder.

At night the men speak to me.
I animate, under their voices
I am intelligent and funny, I have that
fine, smooth skin of women who
never move their faces.

By day the landscape goes by;
there are birds, rocks, other things.
the wind gives us motion or not.

Now that the ship has broken and foundered
on an island, the men
have deserted me to live among the Indians
if they are lucky (their women, quick
with paddles, dressed in vermillion
and minks). I float face-up
in this primeval freshwater bath.

Being alone is a terrible surprise.
It is like landing on the moon.

Look at the world!
There are waxwings overhead and a
shorefull of spruce, pebbles like eggs
in the peacock-coloured water.

What was it the men wanted?
Did they know what they really wanted?

There is one more question
in this series of questions

which is, what do I want
which I never ask, being wooden,
being a decoy
for the next crew,
the next ship, for
whoever will settle
on this perilous water, which is
perfectly clear.

IV THE CAPTAIN WAS KILLED

People said the captain was killed in the surf because
we ran out of red cloth to give them, but it was different.

His arm went up and the rest of him went under, he was
all white and flash. The clothes came floating back
first, the rags we knew so well, a shoe. The wind jumped
up out of the headlands, and all the sails filled over
the wreck with a great noise, like you hear from a crowd
when something happens, an explosion of white sail
and then the wind was blowing the wreck toward whatever
was ahead.

He was cutting bacon for their captain and he sliced off
his fingertip and it bled. The people stared. It was
the final clue, the end of the mystery. Later when he
waded ashore again and demanded men to help repair the
ship, somebody killed him.

He should have told them, maybe they never believed we were gods,
they only wondered how far this windy, ballooning technology
of sails and ship could protect us. Now we want to prove
we are people, we have failures and hopes and women,

but it is too late. We still seem dangerous but now
we are killable.

And now we are here forever. The snow will come in columns.
We can try to say we were just passing through. As a last,
desperate measure, we will try to act like human beings.

V THE ESCAPE OF THE SHIP'S BOY

They sail quickly, nervously along the limestone shores.
Their shell of life is the ship's boat, with four
survivors. They imagine the cracked rock beneath them
to be the remains of cities. They hope to find friendly
aborigines so they can be admired or hated, either one,
but surely one or the other. They are rowing neck and neck
with the new world.

Each night as their boat lays its insecure anchor, dragging
gripless over the smooth paving stones of the bottom,
the men wrestle with dreams. The ship's boy dreams that
someone has stolen his new shoes. The bosun dreams that
a dragoon pistol has gone off in his hand. The cook
dreams that his arms have turned into anchors and the
mate dreams that he is moving a great piano.

(Occasionally in their dreams there are people who come
riding up from the direction of Altair, they are
glassed-in, like church windows, they are all colour and
illumination. And the ones who come from south-west of
Antares are full of words, with prefixes and suffixes,
words of songs in odd music.)

One some days small joys creak out, little joys that fly
loose like young gulls still spotty in their juvenile
feathers. The men say,
    'Look, a headland, around this headland will be the
passage to India.'

On a thin point which seems to float a few inches above
the surface, at a mile's distance, are the people who
inhabit this new world. They are waiting for the men to
do something, something besides row in different directions
and argue with each other.

The aborigines wave, they have built a smoky signal-fire
of green ash. Now the men are startled into the present.
They remember they are here, in the new world, on a body
of water blue as church-glass.

They had been thinking of Cathay, potentates, rescue, silk,
and minor grudges. They want to trade with the aborigines,
explain to them about the great cities that are going to arise
here, they might have given them mirrors so they could look
at themselves instead of out at the world.

The men would have become anxious, and so they began talking
quickly, fetching up words like reassurances, any words.
The aborigines would have become anxious as well, and there-
fore silent. This silence would have made the Bretons
even more nervous, they would have talked faster, sweated
adrenalin (you can smell it), turned to see what the mate
was going to do or think, the mate would have wondered what
the aborigines were going to do or think. Each

human shape either threatens or promises, we cannot stop
to observe who they are, what they look like, if they have souls
or no souls. Quick, move, either they have terrible needs or
we do, one or the other, and one or the other will get
what they want.

White pines seep their resinous odour and gulls with red dots
on their beaks leap up and scream. The ship's boy realizes
there is going to be trouble. The sailors in their fear
suddenly imagine things, a thick-handled fish knife flies
out of somebody's hand.

What in god's name can you be thinking of, the mate yells,
and here we are alone on these shores, beyond us yet another
freshwater ocean, and what have we been dreaming of all
this time? We have not looked at the world in so many years.
Here it is. Shafts of sunlight stalk the water like
immense cranes, the waves are like foil, on their surface
moves the crushed velvet of the wind.

The men pray Christ release us from the terrors of this
unknown continent but they do not mean it. Maybe they want
to be released from each other or themselves but there are
no prayers for this.

In the north-east, a storm, indigo blue and shot with ball
lightning, is under construction. This storm will drive the
rivets from their seating and the ship's boat onto the
stony shore. The ship's boy and all of them turn to the
suddenly building wind. The cook's cheese-paper flies
loose like a message to St-Malo, and all their familiar
lives, unreadable.

I'll run away now and hide, says the ship's boy, while they
fight each other. In his mind he sees himself becoming feral
like the wolf-child of Auvergnon. He dreams of cinnamon factories
and people in the glassy forest who lie down each night
with friendly griffons. The shelves of the new world are
empty of bosuns and mates and cooks.

(But the cities are already here. The streets are here,
laid out in the mind. The mind gropes toward packaging
and barracks and gold mines. The Griffon has already
brought diseases and imported food.

We do not even know what our hands are doing, much less
our feet, as we walk through these tangled mental systems.
But we seem to be moving in a vaguely westerly direction.
We dream, then, of rocky, aboriginal shores.)

Running through stands of cedar, he hears the mate and the
sailors shouting at him. Small darters wing and crackle
in the grass. Ahead in his flight is the legend of the boy
chased by a rolling head, a logic of tangible qualities.
On both sides the beige, flaming foxtail grasses of the
new world race with him, neck and neck.

Somewhere ahead he will have to pay the ferryman, it
will be the Loon, dressed in frost and oils, what the
price will be he doesn't know, he will only want to cross
the water, this water here. The cedar lifts its lacy
hands as if to applaud, but hesitates, shocked by winds.

SONG TO THE RISING SUN (written for radio)
for Caroline Woodward

I

What did we do all winter while we waited for the sun?
It was gone for a long time.
Our thoughts were like seeds in darkness.
What did we do all winter in the Arctic while we
waited for the sun?
The stars never stopped looking down on us.
What did we do as we moved into the precise and surgical
cold of January?
What did we do?
We listened to the radio, we listened to the seductive
and hypnotic voices,
we listened to the voices of pilots overhead in the dark,
we listened for the call sign of the technicians
at the Black Angel Lead and Zinc mine,
we watched with fascination and dread
the talking heads of television from distant places,
we drew up plans,
we cut our losses,
we re-read our contracts,
we visited everybody in the village,
we dreamed,
we were dreamed,
we looked again and again at the southern mountains
where the sun would come up,
we talked ourselves out of arguments,
we deceived each other,
we traded clothes,
we ran the huskies out from under the staff house,
we wrote eyewitness reports,
we wrote appeals to get our friends out of jail in Kuujuac,
we invented relationships,
we became deft and scandalous,
we listened to the breaking noises and the cannonades

39

of the moving ice,
the destruction of ice at the shear zone,
we arose in the dark and saw angels walking with candles
under the landfast ice, through the caves and tunnels
under the landfast ice,
we watched beings walking down from the southern mountains
in glowing zodiacal bituminous fires,
beautiful and shoeless,
we lay back in our beds, starfire descending.
The spirit sings,
the spirit sings,
the spirit also weeps.

II

I have been trying to reach you by radio all winter
but the air is full of darkness,
telepresences, moving stones, talking heads, wizards,
devices, shaky people moving without hands,
devices, radio waves, refuelling aircraft.
I sit up late, listening to Shaman Radio.
The seductive and hypnotic voices tell me of murders
in far places, committed with enthusiasm and skill.
I do not know why the human mind pauses in
the darkness it does.
But mine has as well.
I drink so deeply of this crystalline and windless stillness
but there is no still place for this thirst.

III

When I first came up here
I came up in a Twin Otter, a cargo plane
carrying four barrels of aviation fuel.
I like living on the edge.
We flew over the Black Angel Lead and Zinc mine
at 8,000 feet,
and the stories the pilot told me were always

full of money.
Junk is lethal.
We flew through a thickening, dirty pollution haze
that comes up from the megacities.
Junk is lethal.
He said once his cargo door flew open and he lost
all these boxes of apples
over the Davis Straits,
and he said, you know,
I think Big Stuff will save us.

IV

I am trying to reach you by radio.
Listen. Take thought, take thought, think. Listen. Watch.
I am trying to reach you by radio-telephone,
waiting for the sun to come back.
I wanted to tell you
we don't have very long.
We are losing things.
There is a black hole in the blue world
out of which lost things are going.
We dreamed.
We were dreamed.
There are 100 million tons of sulphur dioxide
staining the polar air
into a haze that pilots cannot fly through.

Junk is lethal.
We are waiting out the long Arctic night.
The air is overloaded with signals.
Brand names, long wave, short wave, the morse of
supply ships coming up the Davis Strait with their cargoes
of summer fuel
and dreaming sailors
dreaming up the long straits
and the heart's charged cargo spills the entire load out
8,000 feet over the Davis Strait

spilling its dirty hearts.
Junk is lethal.
Junk is lethal.

Wake up and start again.
Wake up and free yourself.
You must be told this over and over, in dreams,
in messages, in radio waves.
There is more than this, even though the darkness
is seductive with points of light,
snow refractions,
even though there are angels walking under the landfast ice;
you are sick with power
you are sick with the deep acids of power
heavy metals washing ashore
even though there are beautiful and shoeless people
moving in bituminous fires through the aurora borealis,
even though the legendary stars move in circles
around the high, centred polestar,
there is more than this. There is more than this long night.
You must be told this over and over.
Wake up. Wake up. Look to the southern mountains
look beyond the river of Salluit,
look beyond the Kuujuak, the Povungnirtuk,
Big Stuff will not save us. Wake up. Look. Keep watch.

V

You were promised something. You were promised
something at your birth.
You were promised that the sun would come back
out of the long Arctic night.
You were promised clear air, and clean water.
Listen to Shaman Radio, listen
to this seductive and hypnotic voice;
they promised you the way the sun makes promises
to the moon
even when the moon is on the opposite side of the world

even when the moon has gone down into the running stains
of the Black Angel Lead and Zinc mine
even though the sun has abandoned us and left us
in darkness for so long.
Promises like the cheerful kisses
of the saffron poppies of the Ungava.
Trust yourself, says the invisible sun, trust me
trust the light that may rise within you all winter
time after time
following the route of the invisible sun
and the moon our representative
the refuelling aircraft landing on the sea ice,
trust yourself and the light that may be
rising within you,
beautiful and shoeless
down the long alleys of ice at the shear zone,
in the glitter of accumulated village snow;

everything I saw in the Arctic and everything I did
became a part of me.
This is my body of darkness and this is my cargo of light.
I was heavy with my body of darkness,
I ride with my cargo of light.

VI

And what are the standards set for this sunlight
that has been promised us?
That it be clear.
That it be freely given.
That it fall on everybody at the same time.
That it open our hearts of darkness.
That it illuminate the caves under the landfast ice.
That it give solar power to angels.
That it rise instantaneously over the rim
of the southern mountains,
that it burst like floodwater down the fjord,
that it set alight and inflame the broken ice at the shear zone,

that it repair and mend our angry, flaccid little hearts,
that it ignite the plankton under the sea ice,
that it make poppies flare and glitter on the stone tundra,
that it bring the huskies out from under the staff house,
that it draw the birds forward on their great migrations,
that it signal the caribou of the dwindling Ungava herd
that they shake themselves,
that the hair fly up around them in a bright, luminous cloud
as they shake themselves
and prepare to cross the rapids of the Kuujuak
that it turn on cloud-shadows over the opening sea,
that it awaken love, and foxes.
These are the standards for sunlight.

VII

And so we drift out of the precise, surgical cold of January.
We had been dreamed alive,
out of the wreck of the future
out of the violence of opposites
our dreams washing over us like the tides
under the landfast ice,
rising and falling in secret, glittering caves,
running up the Ungava coast in foam and black salt
the routines of oppressive and heavy metals
the heavy metals now in our flesh
now and forever in our flesh
and in the flesh of our people
and in the flesh of the animals we have dreamed.

VIII

(We always knew we were somebody else
as well as the people we have become.
Something is dreaming us, as persons of intelligent purity,
an evocative and spontaneous self;
we would like to meet this self
in a landscape with Arctic herb-willow blossoms

and the saffron northern poppies
and peregrine falcons overhead
their airy voices light as shortwave,
walking through these dreams in mortal terror
here on the planet of our birth
here in this polar region;
we live through profound experiences
every moment of our lives
every second of our lives,
and we do not know it.
You are right to live in fear, or awe.)

IX

We have to walk on earth as if we lived here.
There is no help for it.
With great relief we learn
we are an animal on this planet.
In the hot moonlight and drifting black shadows,
you are right to live in joy.

X

Every dream is an explorer's map recovered at great cost,
and every map is a chart for land-dancing,
and every river is a song driven by longing.
Be still. Sit down here beside me.
Look at the southern mountains
because this is the opening chord of the music,
because even the darkest heart can be opened
because the sun can arise in the south without our help,
because the only changes we have made here
have been the wrong ones,
because we have torn a hole in the fabric of the past
because we are pouring out 100 million tons
of sulphur dioxide a year,
because we have soaked the pole in a pollution haze
that pilots cannot fly through,

because we have blamed it on everybody else,
because this Arctic sun will open your body on its rising
because your heart is the sun of the world,
because the sun rises and rises over the bare mountains,
the tundra,
the iron cross on the mountain of Salluit,
because the peregrine falcons are coming back,
their airy voices light as shortwave
because I am trying to reach you by radio
and because in the heart of this midnight
there is a sun of the upper air,
because of the bituminous fires, the beings beautiful
and footloose,
because the sun is arriving, igniting the bright
ice of the fjord,
because it was promised us that it would rise,
because we were torn apart into lightness
and dark in our original natures,
because we were torn in half,
because the rising recreates us,
because the rising recreates us
just this second
and no more.

MOROCCAN JOURNEY (written for radio)

The Women's Chorus

This is the story of Ahmad; listen.
Ahmad got caught in the middle of a clan feud
between the Al-Waryaghira and the Ait-Wasised.
He saved his life by running into a house
and laying his hand on the handmill
under the protection of the woman of the house,
and he stayed there for three days.
This was how he saved his life.
Before Islam came here, the people worshipped a sheep.
A sheep! Imagine! A sheep, and Emmama-ni, the goddess
of ruined cities and strayed people, and sign-painters.
We have lots of stories like this,
not all of them have happy endings.
But yours will, Nasrani. If there is somebody left alive
to tell the story,
then that is a happy ending.

Now listen; Ahmad. That was one story.
The other is that there is a saint on the mountain,
Jbil Hmam,
and some other Nasranis came through here once.
They laughed when we told them about the miracles
he did for people.
They laughed! And then they got sick.
One of them died.
Have you been laughing at saints, Nasrani?
Hmmmmm? Have you been laughing at saints?

The Traveller

Walking east, and then northeast,
we came into the mountains.
And every day we walked further into the secret hemisphere
and every day our loads grew heavier.

And every night in the village taverns the men
played at a game,
on a board, around the fire,
moving pieces on a board.
So we walked on, into the Rif mountains of
northern Morocco, toward Ketama.
We went through Bab Taza, and Meknoul and Bab Berrad.
I put down my pack wherever I found some space;
there was space everywhere.
We travelled and got thinner.
It was Ramadan, the new moon like the jewel of Islam,
but it was a thin moon.
Rahmin, bring me a drink of water.
Men sat before the candle flames,
moving small pieces over a board;
they were charting my journey to Ketama.
We were pieces moved on a board,
farther into the mountains,
and every day our loads got stranger and stranger.

I said,
    'Is there a truck going by here to Ketama?'
and they said,
    'Maybe. Maybe tomorrow. There might be an onion truck.'

A second stranger began to walk beside me,
it was a wild, dreamlike fever.
Snow drove through the holly trees
and the mountains were like silk prints
and it seemed the teapot began to tell stories,
steamy and dreaming.

The Women's Chorus

This all depends on time
and time depends on geography
and geography depends on gravity
and gravity is what keeps the evil people down in hell

from floating up like mean balloons.
The soldiers come by, looking for bribes,
and so we dynamite the roads leading into these mountains.
You are in another world, Nasrani.
The helicopters come over, looking for hashish.
The helicopters are heavy, and sometimes
they crash.
But angels and strangers are light,
light as fever, as typhoid.
We will weigh you down.
We will weigh you down with the sound of a flute
and the stories of wars, and marriages,
and betrayals and sorcery.
We sell hashish by the kilogram.
We use it for magic, to poison enemies and to get dreams.
They say the Nasrani use it for fun.
Is this true?
For fun?

The Traveller

I didn't know whether I was going to make it to Ketama
or not. I was worn out with travelling. But we were so far
into the maze of this world there was no way out but back the
way we had come, and that was a very long way. And I thought,
well, you know, everybody has their own geography somewhere,
unfolding from inside themselves, their own planet, and
across these planets there are always strangers, walking,
carrying their stories.

The Men's Chorus

Some people say the world is a china plate,
held up by dragons.
Some people say the world is an egg,
always generating things and the seeds of things to come.
Others say the world is suspended in the mind of
Emmama-ni, goddess of ruined cities and dental work,

divinity of lost causes and sign-painters.
Some people say the world is perfectly full,
a world without strangers or angels or bandits,
peppered over with stars,
bounced through history by a giant
who is perpetually blind drunk.
Geography supplies us with free gravity
and keeps strangers on the surface of the earth
as they travel across it
and it keeps all those evil people from floating
up from hell
like mean balloons.

A Man's Voice; The Headman

No, she can't go any further. You can see she can't go any
further. She has either a fever or an attack of sorcery.
She will stay here until she can travel. Here is Rahmin,
and Fatima Henna, who does people's hair and makes
designs on the hands. And Kenza and Aziza, they will take
care of her in the women's compound. If she goes on she
will die, and so she will stay here and that's all there
is to it.

The Traveller

I was born under a lucky sign. I carried it with me into the
mountains of northern Morocco like an astral umbrella, into the
Rif mountains, the blad-s-siba, the land of dissidence, and
fighting, where people carry their tribal stories like
umbrellas, and the runners slide through the holly and beech
trees with loads of hashish, mysterious and remote.

They said,
   'Don't go there, the mountain tribes are barbarians!'
They said,
   'You'll never come back alive!'
They said,

'Those people used to worship a sheep, or some goddess
called Emmama-na!'
And so, I had to go. I was born under a lucky sign, the sign
of the traveller.

The Women's Chorus

We are Berber, we were once the barbarians
at the gates of the city of Nkur,
a city people only sometimes remember.
We have become blad-s-siba, the land
of fighting and dissidence and tribal wars.
All those people do is fight each other!
Usually over women.

The Traveller

I was born under a lucky sign, the sign of Aries and fire
and fever. I sit, wrapped in homespun cloaks, in the
women's compound, and all my bones glow like phosphorescent
candy. I sit and watch the life of the compound of Mikki
Mohammed, in the mountains near Ketama, with the light snow
falling, and the cow eating pomegranate rinds, and the
geese in the straw. The women are boiling my clothes in a
copper pot, talking. The snow drifts down, making crisp
noises on the fire.

The Women's Chorus

Oh Fatima Henna, where have you been?
Sister, we have not seen you in so long.
We have so many things to tell you.
There have been births and deaths and marriages,
and the tribes, the Al-Waryaghira and the Ait-Wasised
have fallen to fighting, arguing among themselves.
Their sisters and our sisters arguing,
fighting at the women's market.
Somebody got slammed with a petrol tin.

A gun went off.
Ahmad ran into a house and put his hand on the handmill.
Everybody married the wrong people
and then made up songs about it.
Love lost, love gained, love bought, eluded, betrayed,
broken, refused, betrayed, betrayed.
He was a great man, Abdul-Al-Karim, but he was betrayed.

Men's Chorus

And others say the world is an egg, regenerating things,
one thing unfolding, another thing unfolding.
These are the ten most beautiful things;
soap, and henna, and silk,
the plow, and flocks of sheep and swarms of bees
and then the sun and the crescent moon
and horses and books.
These are the ten most beautiful things.

The Traveller
Rahmin, bring me a drink of water.

The Women's Chorus

A sheep, and Emmama-ni,
the sheep-headed goddess who lives
under the cooking pots, and drinks the broth,
who lives under the teapots and whispers stories
about her ancient city of Nkur
and makes mischief
and gives people fevers.
Emmama-ni, hiding in the fire and the handmills,
dreaming, ecstatic, old.

The Traveller

The mind moves where it wants to and when
the mind sits down in a warm dry place

the mind heats up its drum
the mind sits beside a window
the mind walks out at sunrise
like a water-spider
the mind moves where it wants to and when;
there are lanterns and fountains in the land of the Almohades
under the Mountain of Doves.

The Women's Chorus

Walk back and go to sleep again, Nasrani,
what we do here is none of your business.
We are arranging marriages.
It is a delicate and complex work,
and you have seen of course that Mikki Mohammed
has put aside his good wife for another woman,
that flashy bitch from Bab Taza,
and we are plotting mischief
against Mikki Mohammed.
We will transfer the fever from you to him.
Now go away, we are making trouble. Hurry up! Go go go go.

The Traveller

What would we do without strangers?
There are many uses for strangers.
If we did not have them, we would be too much
with each other, we would become tiny and hard.
We would know everything there is to know
and then the world would become perfectly full,
a tight shell peppered over with stars,
and everything would become perfectly known.
The world inside our heads would become so full
of perfectly known things
that it would start to fray out and ravel
and then gravity would give way
and the evil people would start floating up from hell
like mean balloons.

They have taken away my fever
and kept it for themselves.
There are always uses for fevers;
and tin cans, bits of string, scraps of leather . . .

The Women's Chorus

Now go away, Nasrani. We are making trouble, go away.

The Traveller
Rahmin, bring me a drink of water.

The Men's Chorus

And some people say the world is held together
by conflicting forces:
hashish runners sliding through the thickets of holly
helicopters falling toward the fields,
road explosions.
The tribes fell to fighting over the hashish money,
the Al-Waryaghira and the Ait-Wasised,
but it has always been this way, since the age
of paradise, the age of iron after that,
the age of clay pots, the age of vegetables,
and then the age of torch singers and cheap jewelry.
And the age of internal combustion engines,
the age of carbonated drinks,
and the age of the French, with gunpowder
and plastic and gas.
Abdul-Al Karim-Al Khattabi was a great man,
but he was betrayed.

The Traveller

My fever is leaving me,
a stranger going off somewhere.

A Man's Voice
Rahmin, Rahmin . . .

The Traveller

I have been watching Mikki Mohammed.
It seems to me he isn't well.
He stands outside the women's compound, looking thin.

A Man's Voice
Rahmin, bring me a drink of water . . .

The Traveller

Will Mikki Mohammed go back to his good wife
and leave that flashy bitch from Bab Taza?
Will Rashid marry Fatima Henna after all?
Does Rahmin know that Kenza is going to sell the cow?
The women tell me in French that when I go home
to my country, nobody will marry me, because
I am too thin.
And so Kenza and Fatima Henna are making me
a surprise present,
a thick long dress, peppered over with stars,
which will make me look fat.
I have left them everything; my watch
and my gold earrings, my paper
and pens.
I came through the age of iron,
and clay pots, and vegetables,
and torch singers, and now
I will get on an airplane out of Casablanca
the age of
internal combustion engines.

The Women's Chorus

Have you been laughing at saints, Nasrani? Have you
been laughing at saints?

The Traveller

The mind moves where it wants to and when.
The mind sits down in a warm dry place.
The mind heats up its drum.
The mind walks out at sunrise
walking down the Silk Road
the mind is a water-spider, unspinning its tales
one inside the other
and another one inside that and
another one inside that . . .

ONE SISTER
(for Sunny)

One sister will always be fat and the other one thin.
One sister will look good in yellow and the other one won't,
and the one who doesn't look good in yellow
won't be able to carry a tune, either.
Who took my yellow dress?
Who borrowed my blue shoes?
Susan Marie, you took my 100 percent real silk scarf
and you didn't even ask me if you could borrow it!
Amanda Jean got in my diary and read it,
and anybody who gets in somebody else's diary
deserves anything they get.

There will always be one sister who isn't good at math
and one who has wide feet
The one who has wide feet will be the one
who discovers the drop of blood on the stairs

near the woodstove
it will be she who knows
that, if you pour wine on it,
the drop of blood will speak
and name the murderer.

One sister will cover for the other one
when the wrong prince shows up, pimply and alcoholic,
with a glass slipper.

There will always be one sister
who betrays the other ones.
Ah, we know whose fault it is.
It's always somebody else's fault;
it's the one who is good at math,
she just can't find her path in life,
she has to work in this roadhouse
carrying trays of beer,
and the other sisters will tell you
how she used to sleepwalk in the night,
and was once found walking down the railroad tracks
taking some matches to her daddy
who was a brakeman at that time
for the Missouri, Kansas and Texas railroad.

One sister will get divorced and the other one
will stay married forever
and the third one will never get married at all
and will charge a lot of clothes to her account
at a big downtown store.
Dad will always have loved one best
and disliked one most,
and then there was the baby of the family.

One sister will get married and divorced
and have a love affair in fifteen minutes
flat from a standing start,
and the other will take all day to find her hairpins.

Only to discover they're all in her hair.
One sister will, at some time in her life,
yell at the other ones,
'You ruined my life! All of you! You made
my childhood totally miserable!'

Then there is the sister who has no sisters,
and, in fact, makes them up.
She invents for herself all of the above scenes.
For her, books will open up like wicker trunks
full of things she already knew were there
but couldn't get at
until now.
Look, it is a delicate cloth,
and very old.

One sister will travel to foreign places and see
the Tower of London and the other will take a course
in Mary Kay cosmetics, and then lose all her receipts.
'I never had much luck,' she says, on her porch
in Carter country, as she fans herself with a Jesus fan.
One sister will always have had to ride the mule,
while the other will get to take Mama's saddle horse.
The two of them go for the mail like this,
arguing fiercely all the way down Pike Creek road.
'Fair!'
'Unfair!'
'Fair!'
'Unfair!'
Sisters argue like Philadelphia lawyers.

One sister will explain her life in terms of men,
what they have done to her, what they haven't
done to her,
what she wishes they would do to her,
or with her, or without her,
and the other sister will listen angrily,
tapping her fingers on the tablecloth.

But they are trying so hard to get along,
so the one who is doing the little number
on the tablecloth gets up to make more coffee
and thinks,
'She's *still* talking about men.'

This kind of thing will always divide the sisters
a little, even if
they don't know it.
Zinnias loom with accurate brown looks
out of the garden, and their hairdos steam
in the hot sun.
One sister will just have come back from an
assignment in a strange place; there are stamps
in weird scripts all over her passport.
The other one sings in the choir, dazzled by notes.
Why is everybody getting divorced all of a sudden?
It must be something in the water,
says the other sister,
the one with the zinnia hairdo.
And another sister swims across the bay, held up
by blue water. Her sister is drinking
quietly and desperately and continuously
in a northern oil town
and one of her children has fallen off the window ledge.
So the other sister swims with slow determination
from one end of the bay to the other.
It is a matter of liquids.
It is a matter of being held up,
it is a matter of not falling,
it is a matter of keeping on with the swimming motions.

The last sister is the muse who knows
your secret rooms full of jewels, the
one who lives under the teapot, who comes
and goes in the steam.
You don't remember me, she says. *But I remember you.*
They say she lives on the other side

of the mountains. They say she lives
in the ruins of fallen cities and all-night cafes.

She calls you up at one in the morning, collect.
I saw her yesterday at the Salvation Army,
trying on shoes that were both too big,
and too small for her.
Every time I see her, she arrives with the news
of starships. *You don't remember me,* she says,
arriving with a poem,
but I remember you.

A TOURIST EXCURSION TO THE BADLANDS
for Jim
Montana, 1989

On The Way

Along the way there are advertisements insisting
that you do something; eat, or surrender, or back
off from the bluffs, sleep, go forward,
undress, invest in something, catch a flight
to Minneapolis or Butte, have an adventure
in an abandoned mining town.
Take heart; ahead is the REPTILE GARDENS
and the apple, and the expulsion
and the whole damn show.

Along the way are cattle sales;
the panicked ranchy calves
with similar big eyes all looking in double units
the auctioneer searching the crowd of hats
for converts, riders back in the pens wearing
antennae on their galloping heads.
You ask yourself, will I never get
to the Badlands, or the REPTILE GARDENS,
with all the distractions and the fooling around?

and on your way to the Badlands every night
you can stop at western bars, change sliding down
the old walnut counters like lost silver children,
chased by army-coloured pennies, you can
listen to the heavy and soft musician's weapons
of melody and chord,
playing out their hidden agenda.

The musicians work harder at their art
than I ever in my life have worked at poetry;
they take more personal risks and are paid
about the same, all told;

all told, we are handtooled by life and its graving
instruments, marked by odd, random designs
which can't possible mean anything
unless seen from an altitude of 1,000 feet,

and so sometimes our lives look like a REPTILE GARDEN
a roadside attraction on the way to
Hell's Half Acre.

Park Service Brochures

Grey clouds go running by, herded
by thunder, ruined and torn,
sunlight flashes out from between them
as if somebody were throwing it out of a drawer.
As if the chest of drawers were in an empty room
and the room were in an abandoned house
the colour of brushed steel
and the high Dakota wind were banging the doors shut
and open and shut again,
bouncing styrofoam cups hellbent for Apocalypse.

I dreamed last night
you lay beside me
and said, 'Honey, I'm going back

to Corpus Christi.'
And I will go with you; we will
be travellers in hats like flying minds
on their way to *les liaisons dangereux*.

And at the entrance to the Badlands
the Park Service has left brochures
with the names they give this canted earth
and its layering business, describing
the way whole gullies have sat down
to rest on the bones below;
— and this is the extract of vermillion
—this is the aperture of the world's eyebone
   spying out at the ridges of baking powder

with their ash icing and red 'Happy Birthday Dear Badlands'
stripes on them,
the gold sequin parts shaped like ovens
like people hoarding unspent light
unliving their lives in the pressure of dark talk
who try and try to unshutter
and who are looking for the Goodlands.

People who, after all the divorces and the wars,
have been silly and delighted and spendthrift,
forgetting their birthdays,
losing their way home from foreign countries
who get into cul-de-sacs and desert highways,
who pray without thought to whatever divinity
comes along,
She Who Looks Like A Soft Touch, The One Who
Appears The Most Tender-Hearted,
He Who Has The Most Coins In His Pockets,
The Trio who will get you through the REPTILE GARDENS
and the stretches of bony country;
but we are already in it, and what
pressures forced us here, what gambles?

Let us suppose we are people walking across the Badlands.
We are indeed those people walking across
the Badlands,
watching the pearly ridges of buff and opal for hawks,
pulling all our lives behind us, baggage trains,
we are full of plans and calculations
how to get out of here;
I have come so far in my life
and have loved little but my life
until now,
and I think I will begin to rain on this place
until I am empty
or it gives over.

The Goodlands

YOU ARE HERE →• aren't you?
And from here you must invent the Goodlands
because there is no other place to go,
unless we are going to just sull up,
like a calf in the pens, jammed up in the
crowding-alleys,
we have to keep on and walk out of the
bad standing water rimmed with alkali,

toward a river in its own alluvial body
between two sets of mountains,
the Wind Rivers, the Bighorns,
a valley with swales and the weird batty machinery
of ducks going through the air like roaching shears,
and all the paths along the river
plated with October leaves, the salt cedar
yellow as Crayolas,

cottonwoods throwing their leaves of large denomination
out over the crowded world, as if the Pope of Jupiter
would arrive in a Starmobile and bless
the bowing peasant grass,

all the grass of the valley and the benches,
the buffalo grass and the little short grasses
with curly starter knobs, and the
level-headed grasses holding up gemwork stems,
and the tall ones in the swales,
also bowing, wet-footed;

your mind is a nation, populated with standing armies,
post offices, reptile gardens; and some parts are
a wilderness and other parts are dark as railroad clinkers,
and parts are a valley like this, where we are going,
dreaming about going home;
we walk into this clean world,
printing our same bootmarks, careful
as naked people waiting for the
organizations of angels who would drive
us from this discovery, the valley
of the Little Big Horn.

Many people have died to hold this place.
They are still finding pieces of coin and horse
in Medicine Tail Coulee.
But this is why we eat and keep up our strength,
to cross into Montana, like people
without papers or reasons, without a fixed address,
people at large, expendable nomads,
jingling with coins and horses,
into the valley of the Little Big Horn,
thinking we could have dinner here.
We could win this time.

ZERELDA (The mother of Frank and Jesse James)

I

She, like all the best people, came from Kentucky;
she is on her third husband and has never been
happy since the first one died in California,
preaching the Word of God, or maybe
he was panning gold himself, who know?
A Reverend Robert James, sick and Biblical,
passed away on
    the 22nd inst. of this year 1850
    and with his penultimate breath said
    I am far from Zerelda and my boys God keep them
et cetera and then shuffled off this mortal coil
(which appears to be a sort of clay snake)
having never in his life
entered a bar or tavern
sworn out loud, read salacious literature or
fired a shot in anger.

II

Here are her sons, Jesse and Frank, like
small consolation prizes out of
the goldfields;
they are her own, at least so far.
She can neither vote nor sit on a jury
nor go around without the ironclad corsets
or speak aloud of anything she knows to be true;
she is alive and yet without
a legal existence.
The law does not allow her husband to beat her
with a cane any thicker than his thumb.
So she will get another husband
who is smaller, whose thumbs
are not so big.

III

Huge emotions sweep over Zerelda,
tornadoes and electrical storms. The Civil War
was made for people like Zerelda.
She does not even resist, but sails off
like a barn roof.
   They are simple emotions;
   rage, fear, a desire to be noticed.
In her mouth human speech becomes a skinning knife:
They're going to take our niggers away
They think they're better than we are;
   and so on.
She flies into an uncontrollable rage at the mill
she thinks she's been cheated, she goes after
George William Liddle with a potato spade.
   (Can you imagine Zerelda dancing? Can you
   imagine Zerelda seventeen years old
   and dancing in Kentucky?)

IV

At the end of the line of wagons at the mill
there is a black woman with two sacks of field corn
and a jar of zinnias. She will take the zinnias to
her mother if she can.
The woman sees the conflict coming and backs
the mules.
'Sshh-back, sshh-back,' she says,
and the zinnias nod as if they saw the conflict
coming.
She has to get the field corn ground and back home
in good time or god knows.
The woman is owned by a man named Billy Garshade
who lives at Cracker Neck and grows sorghum
and milo.

COLORED RECRUITS!! $100 BOUNTY OR PAY NOT
EXCEEDING $300 TO LOYAL OWNERS!!
The mules back up against the singletree
and the trace-chains crash with a noise like water
or hope. She can easily
imagine herself dancing.

V

The boys don't like to see their mother cheated,
they believe her, they have always believed her,
and now it is Civil War
down the road comes a troop of local Union militia
in blue uniforms;
leading them is George William Liddle.

VI

Frank has already joined the guerrillas
Jesse is fifteen and plowing in the field
when the Union mounted infantry ride in,
they shut Zerelda up like the whole neighbourhood
secretly wished somebody would shut her up,
with a rifle butt;
they find Jesse at the plow and beat him
half to death with the reins.
This is called Civil War.
Enormous thoughts or desires crash and
collide with each other, systems of thought,
ideologies and theories;
Zerelda is screaming, of course,
they will finally burn her out under
General Order Number Eleven.
   (Can you imagine Zerelda dancing?
   Can you imagine Zerelda seventeen years old and
   dancing in Kentucky?)

VII

As the years go by Zerelda gets more dramatic,
Oh Mother, say the huge famous bandits
they are sick of problems with no solution
look up from your soap-making, Zerelda, stop muttering
to yourself, possessed by rages, cheated, vengeful,
thinking you are in actuality making soap
stop talking to yourself
the larger questions of life are for you as well
down the ladder of summer cumulus, out of the
arctic of noon, out of the cosmic laundry of
gigantic clouds come either death or eternal life.
Detectives throw a bomb in the window,
Archie is killed, Zerelda's hand is blown off
Oh Mother
   (Can you imagine Zerelda dancing?)

VIII

Zerelda learns to make soap, wash clothes,
   clean the lamp chimneys, shovel the ashes
from the fireplace with one hand
   the other is a steel hook
does she appear like a monster-woman
from folk tales or legends?
She is
she didn't get this way by herself
she had help.

FRANK INVITES JESSE TO JOIN HIM IN QUANTRELL'S GUERRILLAS: SEPTEMBER 1862

I am coming back for you, leave the house after
 supper,
meet me at Low Gap, I will come with two horses,
 one in each
hand, they will be striped with darkness and the
 shadow
of deep wells.

We will move like clocks through the night hours.
 We will work
for ourselves and when we like we will be
 unemployed as the
goldenrod and the grass. It is better than owning
 thing, it is
better even than getting elected.

Meet me at Low Gap. I will give you a horse of
 violence and
delight, I will give you a horse of agency and black
 powder.
The world is different than we used to think,
 houses catch fire
more easily than they said, killing is simple,
 dynamite is
also fast. The world around us is made of
 matchsticks and
rye straw.
I am telling you, reality is unstable.

Sit on the rails by the salt spring tonight, I will see
 your
cigarette, wait for me at Low Gap, under the broad
 shoulder
of Rattlesnake Hill, stars spark in the dark roach of
 its
diamond back.

We will not be officially counted and no one will
    have time
to call us by our names.

Only saints and killers know firsthand
the red fragility of the human body,
the low gear- ratio of the human mind.

GUERRILLA WARFARE: MISSOURI 1856-1865

I

It is a war we have invented to our own liking.
It is homemade, off- the- wall,
we have invented many new ideas in our war
with our neighbours;
the new ideas are:
bushwhacking
leading Quakers into ambushes
killing all the men over the age of twelve in any
particular town
(Lawrence, Osceola, Danville, Poplar Bluff)
and throwing people down wells.
Anyway, they are new to us.

Altogether, we make something bigger than one
    alone,
more explosive, a group of men reaching
    critical mass.
We are the atoms of an unstable substance, moving
    toward
fission,
we suddenly fuse and go off.

II

The unarmed federals leaping out of the cattle cars
in Centralia yell stop or something.
Our rifle barrels are hot as pokers
we can't stop ourselves
we are being run by something
that lives in us as if we were an abandoned house.
It is watching and watching out of our eyeholes.

*I don't know what it is or what it wants, but I can tell you
this:*
we don't come natural to it.

III

Frank's house is not abandoned,
after all the killing and escapes he
lays up in a corncrib west of Rocheport
reading the constitutional theories of Robert
    Ingersoll,
fingerprints of grease and black powder marking
    the
hot- lead print.
Bloody Bill and Charlie and Fletcher Taylor are
    suspicious:
they eat their sidemeat and fried mush watching
    him,
they know the only thing
looking out of Frank's eyeholes is Frank.
Leave him alone, says Jesse. *You just have to leave him
    read.*

THE END OF THE WAR: RETURNING FROM AN ATTEMPTED SURRENDER: JUNE 1865

This is the story of how it all started. Of how none
   of this was our
fault. We are trying to get home, telling ourselves
   this story.

We are taking the long way around, Jesse's chest
   wound leaks down his
shirt, it makes his belt stocky, at night we have to
   pour hot water

into his boots before we can get them off, he is
   soaked in fluids,
blood, and plasma, we only had one frying pan and
   Charlie Pitts

lost that. Jesse was riding into Burns's Schoolhouse
   with his hands
in the air, calling out he was coming in to
   surrender. We may be

guerrillas but we knew the etiquette, you're
   supposed to hand in
your sword or something and say, Thank you for
   the lovely war,

we'll do the same for you next time, and they fired.
   The first shot
took off half his middle finger, left hand, the
   second shot got

him in the chest and he went flying backwards out
   of the saddle
and took the bedroll with him. It was him and
   Fletcher Taylor.

Fletcher went back to get him. We laid up for a
   week in a triangular
hogpen somebody had knocked together in the
   corner of a rail fence.

Jesse said he's had it up to here with surrendering,
   if he keeps it
up it'll be the death of him. Then it was a matter of
   getting him

back across the Missouri River, riding on the
   strange sliding action
of the flooding water which was like a long material
   being drawn and

drawn underneath the ferry, the far shore coming
   at us in the night
with a slow, expanding movement. We walked past
   the detachment

of federals on the other side like visiting angels on
   our way to
some other annunciation. Jesse said it made him
   feel shameful

and incontinent to be breathing in two places at
   once and in front
of strangers. Charlie wakes us up too early in the
   mornings, he

has either nightmares or visions, he said he saw this
   giant
guinea hen in the oaks two mornings ago, skulking
   there with

its head bowed, quoting text from Leviticus. `It was
mournful,' he said, `and fearsome.' The worst
   thing about Pitts

is that somebody taught him to play the juice harp.
   Jesse rides
upright now, the wound is shutting itself like a
   bank vault

over his safe and valuable heart, nobody notices the
   rare skeletons
of birds or the sudden hair of milkweed, our pods
   are not broken,

the soul does not float on the octaves of the wind,
   all the wars
and reasons for wars are lost, but we will make up
   our own

reasons. We will make up our own story. At
   Appomattox the federal
government learned its fatal lesson; that anything
   can be solved

by the application of superior force. This is what
   happens to
winners. They begin to believe in winning.

And now the federal government believes in banks.
So do we.
We believe in banks.

JESSE MEETS HIS FUTURE WIFE, ZEE MIMMS

Here she is coming in with medicines, with
   bandages for
his infected life.
She can see everything in this big hole in his
   thoughts.
She can see the faulty reason beating and beating,
the lost causes,
the parts that are missing, the blood and the lungs.

There are things that live inside of wounds;
a certain memory fixed in his body forever,
a hole in the heart of Dixie, just south of his
    breastbone.
It was the last time he ever exposed his heart.
It was the last time he ever put his hands
above his head
except for her.

Every man is owed a wife; wives live in a different
    country,
a country of women without civil wars, or trains, or
    motivations.
They arrive with bandages; he imagines they never
    surrender
except to him.

She will make a design of his life, a quilt pattern
rusty with blood, made up of the rags
of women's dresses.
Log Cabin, Courthouse Steps, the Road to
    California.

He says: Marry me.
He says: I want to be able to stop,
just stop and watch you,
a hawk pouring out of the long prairie air
carrying between your wings a commission from the
    fertile sun
and your soul, which will have to serve for us both
and move through us both
like a wind through the bottom fields

an invisible comb, I will be moved and marked
and finally harvested.
Why don't you marry me, he says. Tend to all these
wars, and the broken thoughts, and the open
    wounds.

WANTED POSTER

Jesse Woodson James: five feet eleven inches tall, brown hair, regulation killer-blue eyes. In photographs appears to be considering shooting the photographer. Does not test out well. Approaches casual strangers in an intimate way and interferes massively in their private lives. Is trapped in the dead hole and neither moves nor changes. Steals horses. Inhabits a discoloured landscape through which only one, treacherous path is known to pass. Has the appearance of many ballistics with a flat trajectory. This man is occupied by an army of scars, tip of middle finger left hand missing, and one large scar on chest which oft has spoken with bloody lips. Is always breaking out afresh. Cultivates a desperado aura and can most often be seen in the penny dreadfuls, spotted regularly in novels, poems, ballads, and folktales. Men claiming to be James can be differentiated from him in that they pose willingly in front of cameras, they make political speeches. These people are not the genuine article and are confused. Jesse James was never confused about anything in his life, which will last exactly thirty-seven years, five months, three days, fourteen hours, and ten minutes.

BANDITS' WIVES

What Zee is doing all these years is a mystery, or
   maybe not so
much mysterious as ignored;
   no different from any other housewife in the
   nineteenth century,
in Missouri
   she has to balance everything carefully, how to
   make Jesse the
centre of her life but yet not become too
   dependent; after all, her
husband's work takes him away from home all the
   time, she has to make

some decisions by herself
> but then on the other hand she can't get too
> independent. Jesse

likes to be the head of the household, you know
> how it is, the money

she spends is not her own, it's not Jesse's either but
> let that go

for now.
> Can you imagine being engaged to a bank
> robber for seven years and

he's your first cousin besides; the marriage was
> fairly quiet.
>
> Oh, well, it's all in the family and those Missouri
> rural clans are

tight.
> Zee never wanted to end up like Belle Starr or
> Cattle Kate or

Poke Alice. Those violent whores are attractive to
> historians but

they are usually diseased or dead after a while, the
> whores I mean,

and besides it's no fun having people spit on your
> skirt.
>
> Zee is a good Missouri girl from the right
> background.
>
> Her life and that of Frank's wife Annie is the
> kind of life you

have to imagine or invent, such as the time
> the chimney fire nearly burnt the house down
> and Zerelda said

you have to pour salt down the chimney! and sent
> Annie up on the roof

with a washpan full of salt and Annie's petticoat
> lace caught on a

nail and it all tore off in a strip and nobody noticed
> it till later.

Frank saw this strip of lace hanging from the roof
> gutter like a celebration,

yes, everybody laughed about it for years. And the time
Frank taught Annie to play poker and so Annie went over to Zee's
house with a pack of cards and taught her, and then Zerelda caught them
playing at gambling and said what the hell are the people at the New
Hope Baptist Church going to think about this? so Zee hid the cards
in one of Jesse's socks and Jesse never did figure out where they came
from. And the time
Zerelda borrowed Annie's little portable sewing machine and never
gave it back no matter how many times Annie asked her for it, and one
night Frank came in and said, *We've got to go to Tennessee, right now,*
get the kids ready, they'd done another bank robbery or something,
so Annie and Zee went over in the middle of the night and got the
sewing machine and hid it in the wagon so they were halfway to Jefferson
City before Zerelda even knew it was gone. When they were going along
in the wagon Annie said, `Well, I guess now I'm as big a robber as you
are, Frank, ha ha ha,' and Frank didn't know what the hell to make of
that. And the time
Jesse and two of the gang were at home doing as little as possible
and Zee said she was feeling like homemade sin with this cold. `Jesse,
give me a hand with the house, would you?' and he did; you talk about

a desperate outlaw doing the dishes, wearing that
    Navy Colt five-shot
revolver, standing at the sink, soap bubbles caught
    in the blond hair
of his forearms, singing `I'm a Good Old Rebel'
    and he said, `Honey, I'll
get the sitting room,' and he lifted both hands
    above his head to straighten
a picture of Dan Patch whereupon Robert Ford
    shot him in the back of the head twice
at close range.

JESSE IS THROWN OUT OF THE NEW HOPE BAPTIST CHURCH

(Founding Preacher, Reverend Robert James)

Minutes of the New Hope Baptist Church
Kearney, Missouri
August 12, 1876

    The covenant of the New Hope Baptist Church
was called for and read.
    A motion that the church get seven spittoons
    for the use of the
congregation.
    Carried.
    It was requested Sister Dixie Thompson be
    excluded from the church;
she being found guilty of dancing. Moved that the
    hand of fellowship
be withdrawn.
    Carried.
    Brother Elias Halloway confessed to having
    made a false impression
and requested forgiveness. He having made suitable
    amends, the question

was considered.

   Forgiveness voted.

   The case of Brother Jesse Woodson James being considered, charges of revelry, robbery, murder, intemperance, and other un-Christian acts being preferred, and he manifesting an impenitent spirit, motion that the hand of fellowship be withdrawn and he be excluded from the church.

   Carried.

   On motion of Brother Hancock, Sister Georgina Williams to be excluded from the fellowship of the church upon charges of walking disorderly and having run off to join the Campbellites.

   Carried.

   After sermon by pastor, the doors of the church were opened to membership. None responded.

   Clerk: Jno Burnett

CONFESSIONS OF GANG MEMBER CHARLIE PITTS, KILLED AT NORTHFIELD, SEPTEMBER 7, 1876

I rode into Northfield, Minnesota, with voices in my head telling me forget it, it's not worth it, but I stopped listening to them ever since these voices I mentioned told me to eat axle grease for my sins when I was ten and I ate it and was damn sorry. Nothing east of Hundred and Two Mile River except big dead chickens and rusty pig snouters nowadays. Upside my head is a strawberry mark big as a dollar. This means I have good luck and foresight and get flashes of things that come up out of the back of my head. Listen to the happy pistols clicking and saying their piece. Nothing makes Jesse so content as shooting people. We got other people living inside us, just under the skin, these inside people are not male nor are they female, they are kind of purple-black like the skins of Spanish onions, and they have the same pearly shine. Last night mine begun to slide out of me through the hole in the top of my head through which so much else has escaped too, when I was looking after my horse Sweet Pea, she had a great big locust thorn stuck in her gums. This onion creature began to get fed on the lantern light and slide out of my person. I would have been struck blind and dumb, I would have went and eat axle grease again. This is the thing makes everybody kill people.

Here we go up to Northfield now, this is us getting close to Northfield. We're going to die here and get shot up until we look like sieves. They're gonna run us into a swamp and yell, Surrender, and one of the Youngers is gonna yell back, We don't surrender much, and it will get writ in a book. I'll never get to tell anybody or any one person what it is makes us kill people. Whatever we get in life is provisional. It will eat you in sections and you will die all at once. This thing has been talking out of my mouth all my life and now I will be hit in that selfsame mouth. People who have messages are struck dumb and folks who don't have a damn thing to talk about never shut up. Oh, god, how I loved shooting people. Me and my onion woulda blown up whole cities if I'da had the gunpowder. I will finally win the argument with the purple-black party inside, which was flying out toward the simple lantern in the barn and Sweet Pea and the world. Leaving me to voices and rye straw. This is Northfield, my Minnesota onion war.

POCKETS

In the pockets of the corpse of Bill Chadwell, killed
    at Northfield,
there was found a map of the Western states, a
    pocket compass, a box
of salve, a Howards gold watch, an article on the
    Yale lock torn from the
local paper, gold sleeve buttons with enamelled
    leaves, and a gold ring.

In the pockets of Bill Miller, killed at Northfield,
    there was found
a gold Waltham watch, ten cents, an advertisement
    for a Halt's safe with
an engraving depicting a robber giving up on trying
    to enter it, and a
business card from a St Peters, Minnesota, livery
    stable.

In the pockets of Charlie Pitts, alias Samuel Wells,
    there was found
five cents, a label from a whiskey bottle, and a
    Spanish onion.

RAISING HOGS

September of 1876 Frank rides quietly away from
    the disaster of Northfield
toward Tennessee like the whole thing was just
embarrassing; everybody dead or captured,
the bank unrobbed, he won't
let Jesse drag him into these things again.
Frank's going to Tennessee and raise hogs
he crosses the river at Cape Girardeau
it's a very hot river town, the Mississippi
is actually steaming,

nobody asks who you are.
He is seduced by all the simple normal people
at the ferry landing, he will send for Annie
and the kids, he is crossing the river into Little Egypt,
he's going into agriculture as if it were a religion,
the Holy Fire Church of Prophecy and Pigs.
There will be peace in Waverly County
they have relatives down there he can count on
never go anyplace you don't have relatives.
It's all in how a man comports himself
walking upright amongst the swine.

FRANK GETS NERVOUS ABOUT JESSE'S KILLER INSTINCTS

You grow blue in the steamy days of July, the
   depths of heat in your
shrunken house in St Jo, blind shadows.

I hear cries, shouts, the final appeals of men
   working out some
predictable destiny in a swamp, out of ammunition,
   crude as ore.
These sounds appear to come from my dreams.

Sometimes you are there, soaked in oak shadows,
   the hard shells of
mental ammunition, green shade moving like
   suspicious neighbours where
next door is always full of armed men, the very
   guinea hens call your
name as if it were the announcement of a fabulous
   act, the very yard
dogs appear quiet and stiff with intent as
   undertakers, nobody pities
your hard, red karma.

This is what was made of you, stuffed into a
 five-button cutaway suit,
the fingers into gloves, arms into the linen shells of
 drover's dusters;
we see you coming a mile off, riding right through
 Clay County and into
folklore, clashing with real federal silver dollars,
 realer than we
have seen in a long, long time.

Through the blackberry and sumac east of
 Otterville, at Rocky Cut,
you get the drop on everybody. Talk about trains.
 It was so daring
and so daylight.

It was too bad about Northfield. If only you had
 asked the right people.
But all along the turnpike behind, here comes our
 long company: Captain
John W. Sheets, D.W. Griffith, Joseph Lee
 Haywood, Frank Wymore, Frank
McMillan, the unarmed federals we were shooting
 three at a time at
Centralia.

What I will answer for is not the federals or the
 bank clerks but that I
came back for you at Low Gap, full of persuasion
 and leading horses.

I cocked you like a pistol, you were efficient and
 fifteen. `And I
said: Oh, that I had wings like a dove! For I would
 fly away and be at
rest. Lo, I would flee far away and live in the
 wilderness.' Psalm 55.

The young men who are joining us now are
   treacherous and don't remember
the war. Something moves and grows in me like an
   apology, a hope, a
mass demonstration. At night when I sleep my
   hands fall each to one side
empty as clothes without people in them. I think
   this is how husbands
are, in their own beds, in their own time.

JESSE: HIDING OUT IN TENNESSEE

He is having an adventure. It is very seductive and thrilling. He has changed names many times now. He is hiding out in Tennessee, a hot night, an old farmhouse, listening to the clock's neurotic metronome, nobody knows where he is. He finds this very moving. He moves through the Tennessee night and nobody knows where he is. He changes names.

He investigates things with complete freedom. He looks into drawers. He is carrying a gun in case somebody interrupts him. He is the secret agent of a great and important cause, the last of the underground Confederate Army, the Dixie Mafia, the End of the World Gang, Everybody down here thinks he is a Mr Howard, and the people in Kentucky thought he was a Mr Woodson, and the people somewhere else will think he is a Mr Hite. Behind all these names is a sentence of death, which he has escaped now three times: once from fright, once from spite, and once from a desire to show off.

All day long people have been looking at him and choosing what to think about him, there have been whispers behind his back, he has nodded amiably at certain statements. But now in the private night his image and impression is not being appropriated by all the daylight people who walk the daylight earth down here in Tennessee. Now nobody knows where he is and so they cannot think about him. Only *he* can think about *them*. He can think about them and watch them from under his hat and choose not to appear to them. He cannot now be robbed of his face or taken to jail or taken aback or think straight. He is not really thinking straight.

It was really just a process of getting rid of his name, and after that his image, and after that his body, and after that his presence. Now what burns in him is match struck at the very centre of his brain or mind. A coal-oil lamp is sucking the thick night air into itself in the middle of the table. It's going to be hot all night long. The coal-oil lamp is hot too but he has to have light to disappear by. He realizes he is going through somebody's desk drawers and he has a revolver in his left hand. He's going through Frank's desk drawers. It's a scene. He's having an adventure. You can't have an adventure unless you have a gun. His wife and children sleep as if they were suspended in spring water and the whippoorwill is releasing note after note in a rain of musical fluid. This is what the adventure is all about, it's about Frank. Frank knows his real name. The moon rises from behind a hill, it focuses on Tennessee and out of the mind of the moon walks a blaze-faced sorrel horse. The devil's trumpet flower opens its red mouth and says, *Yes*. Jesse listens as the horse speaks in the language of human beings. Don't talk back. Don't say anything. Because you have abandoned your daylight self with such urgency and such joy, because nobody knows your name, there is the danger of being absorbed by the language of animals.

He realizes he lives among *vegetables*. The oak forest cover, the tulip trees, the standing field corn all night long hacking and sharpening its coarse leaves, down in the bottom fields under the moon. The Cherokee Bukka-man hacks and sharpens his coarse leaves, down in the bottom fields, all night long. Human slavery never seemed to bother him much. It changes names.

Without an identity he begins to grow huge and to evaporate. He can't sit quietly and watch it happen by the light of a coal-oil lamp. It would be a kind of surrender, here in Tennessee, without a name. Without a name anything can take you over, anything can fill you with its language. In his brother's desk he discovers an envelope; it has a name on it, Dick Liddle, and the return address says Richmond, Missouri; evoking the grubby and restless pleasures of Cracker Neck. Gratified, he puts it back. It is a sign. It is a portent. All this night he has been adventuring around without a name, going to and fro in the earth, walking up and down on it. In Missouri something is waiting, but at least he will have a name for it to happen by. `And not even the angels shall know the hour of his coming.' Back to Clay County, where at least they will have the right name to put on the headstone. All the visions cloud over and then shatter; he blows out the lamp.

YANKEES IN ST LOUIS

I

They go into St Louis on their way back from Tennessee
and stop in a house of ill repute
tending soberly and carefully to their needs.
Sated raptures.
The girls are Irish or at least have no apparent diseases.
It's better than the times around Rocheport and Danville
in 1864. They think, anything is better now than it was
in Rocheport; living in the mud
of the Little Chariton and the spirit will rise
out of the body in spite of everything.
This is what Frank has always counted on.
Frank is always hoping the spirit will rise
out of the body. There were days of nothing
but a kind of sloppy ecstasy, around the river,
sitting on the banks outside Rocheport with the
river rising and rising,
   the simple innocence of adolescence;
   Boys, let's go burn down Danville.

II

They don't want a pardon.
They stroll through an exclusive neighbourhood
dressed soberly in five-button cutaway suits.
There are a lot of rich Yankees around here, says Jesse.
These are not the white-hog Union partisans of Missouri,
these are rich Yankees.
They walk past the Eliot house at 2635 Locust,
on toward the train station at the River.
Jesse says, *What do you bet me, Frank? I bet those people
would spend half a day deciding whether to part their hair
this way or that.* Frank takes his Hamilton watch from
his watch-pocket. *How come they won the fucking war, then,
Jesse?* There is no answer to this at present.

THE IRISH GIRL AT THE PIE DOG HOTEL AND WHORE HOUSE

She has made up stories about the farm and everything, sometimes without even being asked, and decides she doesn't want anything but money anyway. Send out for the evening newspaper, the *Post-Dispatch*. Entertaining news of robberies, men running away with satchels of money. The lace curtains of the Pie Dog Hotel run inward, printing blue shadows, a new edition every second and the men from Tennessee are gone. It will be better in a week more or less when she gets some time off. The light isn't good. That's how things go. They go fast and in a bad light. Again and again the female performers lay on a bed and think about their histories. None of them have good fortune. Or, fortune is for somebody else. Or fortune is for women without any particular talent and so we specialize in men. Will the electric light tan? Dr Edmund Beard says no, it won't. *I love to hear the train coming down the tracks with all its symptoms of wanderlust, its horn like a choirmaster sounding the beginning note for a phantom choir that never sings, running up from the bottomlands of the*

Mississippi, up the Spanish Trace, and the drowned fields of rice and the willow-oak wet and covered with Virginia creeper, the devil's-trumpet vine. Everything passes by the Pie Dog Hotel in the night, cousins and opportunities, the grass waves in little rivers in the wind of the trains' passage even in the St Louis yards. She wishes she were grass like that and disembodied. Not to have a body; to leave it behind entirely. If she could sing she would make up a song; `The Irish Girl's Lament'. She would be all right if it were not for her body lying on its bed. The body is the copperhead in the haybale, on a wicked frosty morning you split the bale and are struck. She is afraid, looking out the window onto Lafayette Street, that the trains will crash and move across the landscape and not come anywhere near her, that nobody will ever speak to her except as they do. There is just a lot of intolerable noise downstairs (but it is not the news of the world but her own noiselessness) and by now she knows enough to move very quickly into the difficult parts.

THE KILLING OF JOHN W. SHEETS, GALLATIN, MISSOURI 1865

This is a stickup:
your money or your life.
We are beginning to understand
they will always choose the money
but a force has been filling Jesse for days, he is
under pressure or water,
he turns at the door of the bank and you could see
his whole soul and the entire static charge
pour out not once but five times.
The Gallatin Farmer's Bank crashed with the noise;
flashes, bangs, hot blue surprises.

Life flies out of the man with his hands up
like air from a balloon.

Jesse's blaze-face sorrel horse bolts and drags him
down the main street of Gallatin
banging his head off the town pump.
I pulled him behind, my horse sank and lunged, carrying
two heavy men and a sack of dollars,
two grown men and a sack full of money.
He said he thought he was going to get blown away
but it was kind of an exciting feeling.

THE TRIAL OF FRANK JAMES 1882

*Governor, I want to hand over to you what no living man
except myself has been permitted to touch since 1861,
and to say I am your prisoner.*

As he lays his pistols down on the governor's
   polished desk
we can see him pausing for the photographer
among the globe lamps, facing the man with the
   black hood
on his head, who is using
an 8 x 11 dry plate with a double plate holder.

We, too, are looking for the right authority
to whom we may hand in pistols we do not have
and confess to robberies we have not committed
and apologize to corpses we have not murdered.
We, too, hope for a trial packed with old confederates.
We expect, like you, to get off scot-free, revealing
little of our lives or personal disasters before
an admiring crowd,
stripped of nothing but our sidearms. You can
always buy more sidearms.

If we too, could find the right one to whom to
   surrender—
but we are choosy—

before whom we could unbuckle everything
and lay down
our old defenses, drop them
on a mahogany desk, and the Authority, looking on
with mild and kindly eyes, would not know
   or would have
forgotten what we have done
   unspeakable things
which now seem like nightmares or war footage.
   And the Authority says, That's okay Frank, or
whatever your name is, it was a typographical error,

you were assigned the wrong parents, the wrong war,
an extra Y chromosome by mistake.

No one ever says I am your prisoner without
believing somehow in clemency, in mercy
   or in short memories, it is
not something said by battered wives or people
held in deep prisons or
   children with cigarette burns.
It is not said
by those who can no longer talk.

THE LAST POEM IN THE SERIES

The scholar who studies the life of Frank and Jesse James
needs solitude.
This person approaches a cabin through fields and some
woods slowly, seriously, as if they were going there
to take vows.
Everything else has flown away.

There are no other people.

The flame shapes of cedar and scrub oak are drawing
something huge and nourishing out of the clay subsoil,

a substance we can only guess at.
Johnson grass burns in its low fires, the colour of prairies.
The sky at this hour and season is a gemmed glass, blue
and refreshing, it has raised our broken sight many times
before this.
In the cabin are the voices of the original angers, plotting
to rob some establishment of all its savings and loans.
They wait.
It is up to the person who wants solitude to abandon them.
If you release them, they will fly off
like birds or trains.
Your skull is very small under the awning of the universe.
All the time you walk toward the cabin
huge electrons are raining down on you out of the heart
of the sun. What do you think of that?
Before you can step in the door, surrender and disarm.
It is a kind of bank, and can be robbed only
by the anti-bandit.

This is the end of the story of Jesse and Frank.
The grass pours by in the white wind like a river
out of the hill country, flooding and breaking,
and you are smoothed by its lengthy currents.

And so you walk in the door of the bank;
your hands are empty.